WHERE THE SUN KISSES THE SEA

By Susan Gabel

Illustrated by
Joanne Bowring

Perspectives Press
P.O. Box 90318
Indianapolis, IN 46290-0318

Perspectives Press
P.O. Box 90318
Indianapolis, IN 46290-0318

Manufactured in the United States
of America

Library of Congress Cataloging-in-Publication Date

Gabel, Susan L. (Susan Lynn), 1956-
   Where the sun kisses the sea.

   Summary: A little boy living in an orphanage dreams
of finding a forever family where all the children share
the same family name.
   [1, Orphans—Fiction.   2. Adoption—Fiction]
I. Bowring, Joanne, ill.   II. Title.
PZ7.G114Wh   1989   [E]   89-16296
ISBN 0-944934-00-5

To my little Ben

Once there was a little almond-eyed, dark-haired boy who lived far away in a land where the sun kisses the sea and the clouds sink into the edge of the sky.

Each evening as he pulled
off his day clothes and
climbed onto his pallet on
the floor nearest the door,
he would whisper sleepily,
"Good night, clouds. You are
sinking into the edge of
the sky. Tomorrow I will
see you again."

Each morning he would awake and say, "Good morning, sun. It is good to see you kissing the sea once again," as he put on his thin leather sandals, pulled his tunic over his head and washed his face and hands in the basin near his room.

This little almond-eyed boy
enjoyed his days playing with
the many other children who
lived in his very large house
by the sun-kissing-the-sea.
There were so many children,
the little boy could not
remember all their names.
Yet, they played together
day after sunny day.

The children would play
running-and-hiding games.

Their favorite place to run and hide was near the water's edge, where Grandfather sat every day. Grandfather was a sight to see, every day sitting on his little bench, with his long white robes, his bald and shiny head, and his scraggly beard. The smallest children would always try to hide under his robes, and he would swoosh them away if they interrupted his meditations.

Often the children would play finding-and-squealing games. These were some of their best times together. The children would run through the small waves on the beach as the water lapped against their ankles. Then, as the water trickled back into the sea, they would find tiny shells and squiggly crabs. The youngest children would pick up the shells and put them in their pouches to save for trading later. The oldest children would catch the crabs and wiggle them in the smallest faces, delighted to hear their high pitched squeals.

The children also played
sitting-and-thinking-up-stories
games. These stories were
scary on dark and rainy
nights. But usually the stories
told about the children's
longing for a family where
they would be tucked to sleep
at night and where they
did not have to share a
grandfather with so many
other children.

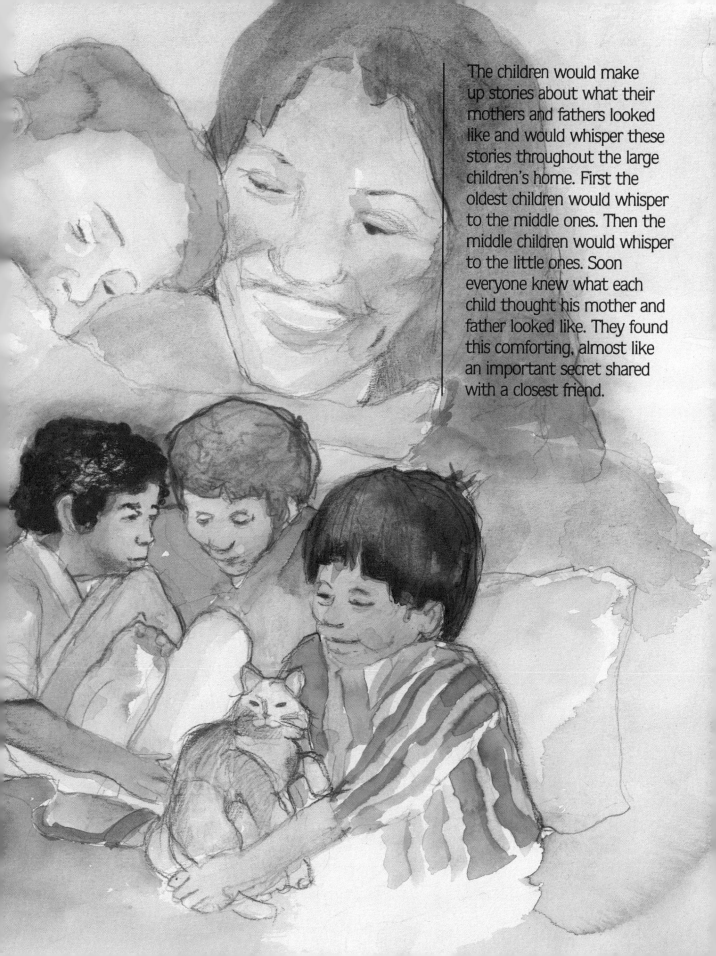

The children would make up stories about what their mothers and fathers looked like and would whisper these stories throughout the large children's home. First the oldest children would whisper to the middle ones. Then the middle children would whisper to the little ones. Soon everyone knew what each child thought his mother and father looked like. They found this comforting, almost like an important secret shared with a closest friend.

The little almond-eyed boy had many happy memories of the playing days with his friends. When he needed a game or a story, he had many friends to help invent new games and many children to whisper secret stories to. But children alone cannot be safe. Grown ups were needed to take care of so many children.

There were many kind and loving grown ups in his very large house, too. There were the nannies who rocked the children to sleep at naptime. Nannies were a favorite grown up for the smallest ones because they would sing soft cooing songs that told of mothers carrying their children on their backs through marketplaces filled with warm, sharp smells.

There were the cooks who made the spicey-best cabbage and the softest, fluffiest white rice. On very special days the cooks would stuff small puffy pastries with fresh fish from the market. This was the little almond-eyed boy's favorite treat.

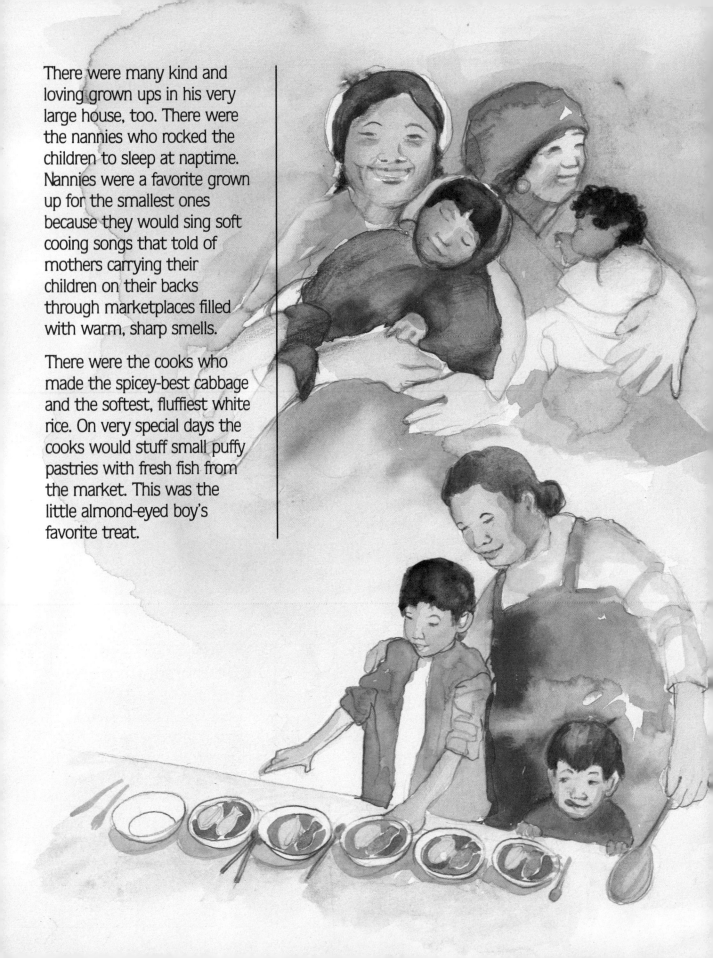

There were the teachers who expected bowing bodies, lowered eyes, and polite answers. Teachers were very strict at the children's home, but their sparkly eyes told of a firm love that a forgetful little one could not erase.

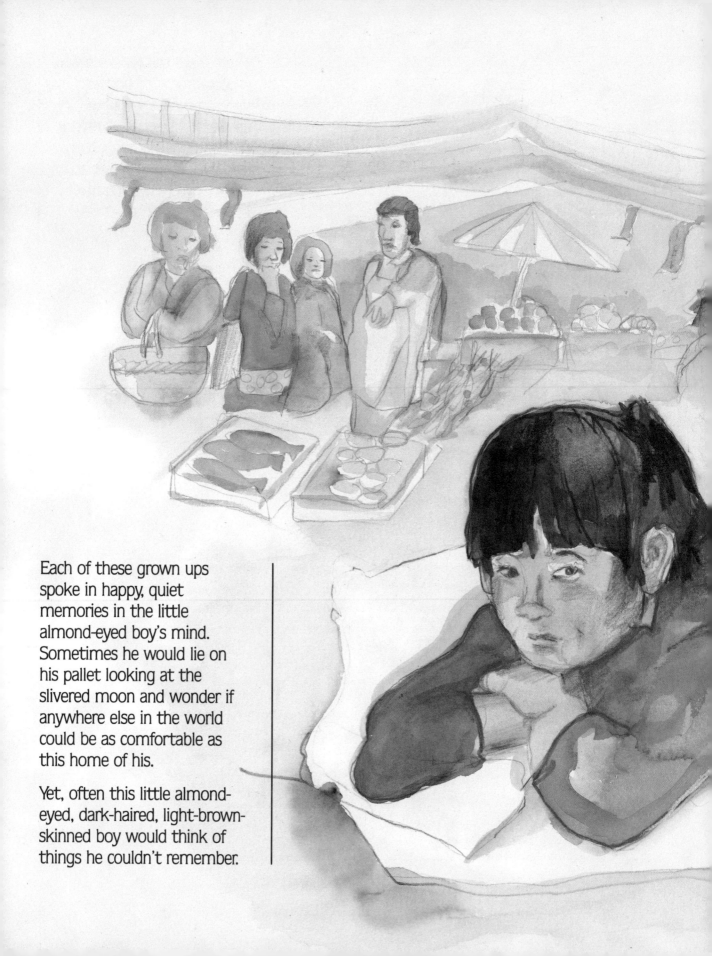

Each of these grown ups spoke in happy, quiet memories in the little almond-eyed boy's mind. Sometimes he would lie on his pallet looking at the slivered moon and wonder if anywhere else in the world could be as comfortable as this home of his.

Yet, often this little almond-eyed, dark-haired, light-brown-skinned boy would think of things he couldn't remember.

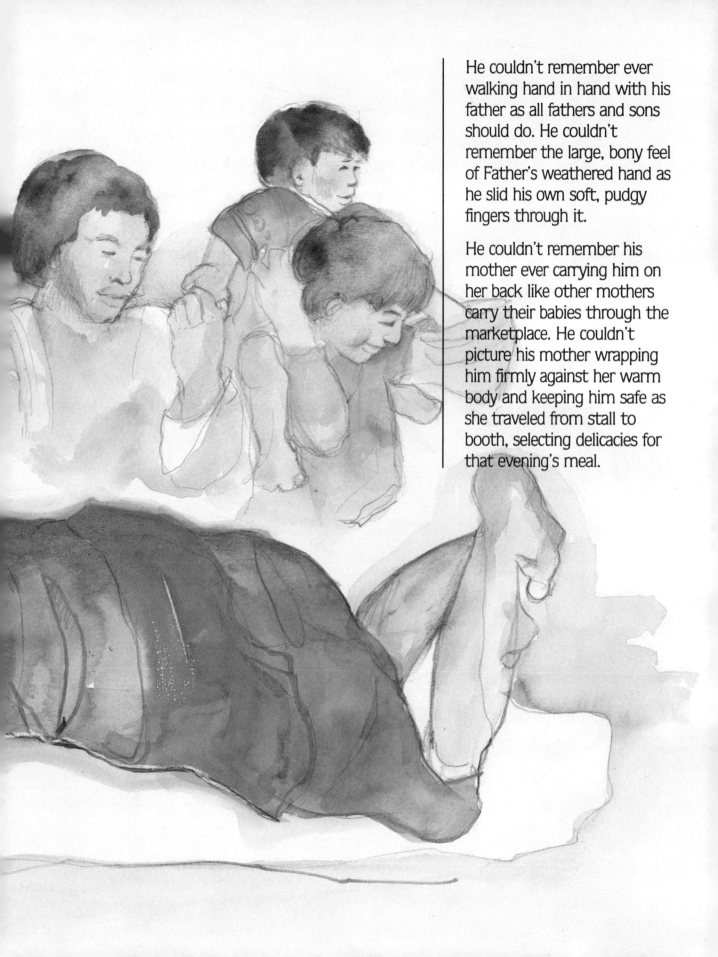

He couldn't remember ever walking hand in hand with his father as all fathers and sons should do. He couldn't remember the large, bony feel of Father's weathered hand as he slid his own soft, pudgy fingers through it.

He couldn't remember his mother ever carrying him on her back like other mothers carry their babies through the marketplace. He couldn't picture his mother wrapping him firmly against her warm body and keeping him safe as she traveled from stall to booth, selecting delicacies for that evening's meal.

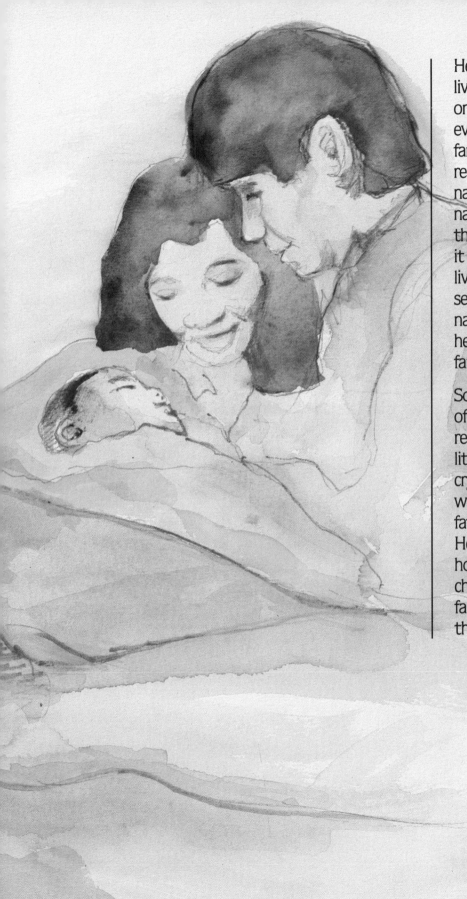

He couldn't remember ever living in a smaller house with only a few children, where everyone shares the same family name. He couldn't even remember what that family name might be. He knew his name was "Lee" and he knew the grandmothers had chosen it for him when he came to live in this big house. Yet, it seemed as if there should be a name out there for him that he could share with his own family.

Sometimes, if these thoughts of things he couldn't remember were too sad, the little almond-eyed boy would cry softly into his pallet. He would cry for the mother and father he couldn't remember. He would cry for the smaller house with only a few children. He would wish for a family where everyone shared the same name.

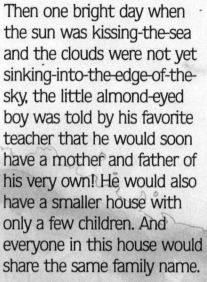

Then one bright day when the sun was kissing-the-sea and the clouds were not yet sinking-into-the-edge-of-the-sky, the little almond-eyed boy was told by his favorite teacher that he would soon have a mother and father of his very own! He would also have a smaller house with only a few children. And everyone in this house would share the same family name.

This was very surprising news! Although this was what he had dreamed for as long as he could remember, the little almond-eyed boy wondered about many things. What did this new mother and father look like? Would they love him like he had hoped? Would the smaller house with only a few children look like the one he dreamed about? What would be their same family name?

Soon, his questions were to be answered. Soon he was on his way to his mother and father and his smaller house with only a few children. Soon he would share their family name. The journey was far and long. First, he boarded a bumpy bus which drove him farther than the little boy thought there was earth. At the end of the bus ride, a very large airplane stood ready to fly him far away. It looked as if he would have to leave his sun-kissing-the-sea and clouds-sinking-into-the-edge-of-the-sky. As the plane rose through the clouds and the sun shone bright into his puddled eyes, the little boy said goodbye to his old sunny friend and waved sadly to the clouds he thought he might never see again.

But when his journey was through, he still saw the sun and the clouds. He was in a new place, one that looked very different from his home by the sea. There was no sea here, only brown soil and green grass. "Perhaps," he thought, "I should call this new home 'where-the-sun-kisses-the-earth-and-the-clouds-sink-into-the-edge-of-the-hills'."

He could still remember the many children who played running and squealing games with him. He could still remember the caring grown ups in his very large house. He could still remember hiding under Grandfather's robes by the water's edge and getting swooshed away. These memories were comforting as he was led through long, noisy halls to a waiting room with too many strangers.

And then, as he was thinking of the memories that he could keep inside as comforting thoughts, he looked up to see his mother and father. "Mommy! Daddy!" called the boy using words from his far away land. He hugged them tightly, hoping they would feel his little body and love him as he had wished.

Mother and father felt his little body and hugged tightly as if they would never let go. They, too, had longed for this day. Quickly, the little almond-eyed boy scurried upon his mother's back and whispered softly into her ear, "I love you" in his sun-kissing-the-sea language. And as he whispered, his mother understood him to say, "I love you" in her own language.

With this special greeting, Mother carried her little boy on her back as all mothers should carry their babies. Father held his son's pudgy hand as all fathers should do. And the three of them went quickly to their house with only a few children, where everyone shared the same family name.

The Author

Susan Gabel, M.Ed., is a parent, an educator, and a writer. She and her husband live in Southfield, Michigan, with their four children, who were adopted. Her family is multi-ethnic, formed through both local and international adoption. Susan was raised in an adoptive family, with a brother and sister adopted as infants. The value of adoption for both adults and children has always been an important issue to her. Her first book, *Filling In The Blanks: A Guided Look At Growing Up Adopted* (Perspectives Press, 1988) is a workbook for 10-14 year old adoptees.

Susan has made several television appearances and written about adoption issues, her topics including waiting children, civil rights issues in adoption, special needs adoptions, and parent-advocacy for children who were adopted. A special education teacher, she holds a B.A. in learning disabilities. Her master's degree is in reading from Wayne State University, Detroit, Michigan. Through the years, she has also been involved with parent training and child advocacy in the field of disabilities. She is currently involved in projects that enable children with disabilities to be accepted within the community. She is a Board member of Community Opportunity Center, a nonprofit agency serving adults with disabilities in Wayne County, Michigan.

The Illustrator

Joanne Bowring and her husband are the parents of a Korean-born daughter, Mary Won Hee, and a son by birth, Timothy. A commercial artist and free lance illustrator working in the Milwaukee, Wisconsin area, Joanne has handled all artists' media including photography, graphics materials and watercolor. She attended Mount Mary College and holds a BA in commercial art from the University of Wisconsin — Stevens Point. She illustrated *Real For Sure Sister* by Ann Angel (Perspectives Press, 1988).

Let Us Introduce Ourselves

Perspectives Press is a narrowly focused publishing company. The materials we produce or distribute all speak to issues related to infertility or to adoption. Our purpose is to promote understanding of these issues and to educate and sensitize those personally experiencing these life situations, professionals who work in infertility and adoption, and the public at large. Perspectives Press titles are never duplicative. We seek out and publish materials that are currently unavailable through traditional sources. Our titles include ...

Our authors have special credentials: they are people whose personal and professional lives provide an interwoven pattern for what they write. If **you** are writing about infertility or adoption, we invite you to contact us with a query letter and stamped, self addressed envelope so that we can send you our writers guidelines and help you determine whether your materials might fit into our publishing plans.

Perspectives on a Grafted Tree

An Adoptor's Advocate

Understanding: A Guide to Impaired Fertility for Family and Friends

Our Baby: A Birth and Adoption Story

The Mulberry Bird: Story of an Adoption

The Miracle Seekers: An Anthology of Infertility

Real For Sure Sister

Filling in the Blanks: A Guided Look at Growing up Adopted

Sweet Grapes: How to Stop Being Infertile and Start Living Again

Perspectives Press
P.O. Box 90318
Indianapolis, IN 46290-0318